HOPSCOTCH
ADVENTURES

Sir Gawain'
and the
Green Knight

by Karen Wallace and Neil Chapman

W
FRANKLIN WATTS

First published in 2009 by
Franklin Watts
338 Euston Road
London
NW1 3BH

Franklin Watts Australia
Level 17/207 Kent Street
Sydney
NSW 2000

A CIP catalogue record for this book is available
from the British Library.

ISBN 978 0 7496 8557 7 (hbk)
ISBN 978 0 7496 8569 0 (pbk)

Series Editor: Jackie Hamley
Series Advisor: Dr Barrie Wade
Series Designer: Peter Scoulding

Printed in China

Franklin Watts is a division of
Hachette Children's Books,
an Hachette UK company
www.hachette.co.uk

King Arthur's court at Camelot was
feasting on New Year's Day.

Suddenly, a giant Green Knight appeared. "I have a challenge," he shouted, holding up an axe. "The bravest man here may strike at my neck once. Next year he must come to me and I will strike at *his* neck."

Sir Gawain, the youngest knight, begged King Arthur to let him accept the challenge.

Arthur agreed and Sir Gawain chopped off the Green Knight's head with one blow.

Then, to everybody's amazement, the Green Knight picked up his head and climbed on his horse!

8

"I'll see you next year," he said
to Sir Gawain as he rode away.

Sir Gawain did not think the Green
Knight would live, but he had
accepted the challenge. So, the
next winter, he went to find him.

Sir Gawain's journey was long and
cold. On Christmas Day, he stopped
at a beautiful castle. The kind lord
and his wife invited him to stay.

Next morning, the lord went hunting. "Let's play a game," he said as he left. "I will give you what I get today if you give me what you get."

When the lord was away, his wife gave Sir Gawain a kiss.

"Here is a deer," said the lord when he returned. "What do you have for me?"

Sir Gawain kept his promise
and gave the lord a kiss.

15

The second day, the lord went hunting again. While he was away, his wife gave Sir Gawain two kisses.

"Here is a boar," said the lord
when he returned home.
"What do you have for me?"
Sir Gawain gave the lord two kisses.

On the third day, the lord went
hunting again. His wife kissed
Sir Gawain three times.

Then she gave him a green, silk
belt. "This is a magic charm.
It will protect you," she said.

When the lord returned, he gave
Sir Gawain a fox. "What do you
have for me?" he asked.

Sir Gawain gave the lord three kisses, but he did not give him the green, silk belt.

On New Year's Day, Sir Gawain found the Green Knight sharpening his axe.

He trembled as he bared his neck. "I'm here to keep my promise," he said.

The Green Knight brought down the axe twice on Sir Gawain's neck, but he didn't hurt him.

The third time, he made a tiny cut.
"Why haven't you killed me?"
cried Sir Gawain.

"I am really Sir Bernlak, the lord of the castle," explained the Green Knight. "I didn't kill you because you told me the truth about Lady Bernlak's kisses.

"I only cut you because you kept the green, silk belt. You were wrong to trust a charm. King Arthur's sister, the witch Morgana, changed me into the Green Knight to test his court!"

Sir Gawain returned home and told his tale. Then all the knights wore green, silk belts like him to show he was the truest, bravest knight in Camelot.

29

Put these pictures in the correct order.
Which event do you think is most important?
Now try writing the story in your own words!

Puzzle 2

1. This belt will keep you safe.

2. My husband has gone out hunting.

3. What am I going to tell the lord?

4. I challenge the bravest man here!

5. Find me next year to keep your word.

6. Let me accept the challenge, King Arthur!

Choose the correct speech bubbles for the characters above. Can you think of any others? Turn over to find the answers.

Answers

Puzzle 1

The correct order is: 1f, 2a, 3e, 4c, 5b, 6d

Puzzle 2

Sir Gawain: 3, 6

Lady Bernlak: 1, 2

The Green Knight: 4, 5

Look out for more Hopscotch Adventures:

TALES OF KING ARTHUR

1. **The Sword in the Stone**
ISBN 978 0 7496 6694 1

2. **Arthur the King**
ISBN 978 0 7496 6695 8

3. **The Round Table**
ISBN 978 0 7496 6697 2

4. **Sir Lancelot and the Ice Castle**
ISBN 978 0 7496 6698 9

5. **Sir Gawain and the Green Knight**
ISBN 978 0 7496 8557 7*
ISBN 978 0 7496 8569 0

6. **Sir Galahad and the Holy Grail**
ISBN 978 0 7496 8558 4*
ISBN 978 0 7496 8570 6

TALES OF ROBIN HOOD

Robin and the Knight
ISBN 978 0 7496 6699 6

Robin and the Monk
ISBN 978 0 7496 6700 9

Robin and the Silver Arrow
ISBN 978 0 7496 6703 0

Robin and the Friar
ISBN 978 0 7496 6702 3

Robin and the Butcher
ISBN 978 0 7496 8555 3*
ISBN 978 0 7496 8568 3

Robin and Maid Marian
ISBN 978 0 7496 8556 0*
ISBN 978 0 7496 8567 6

TALES OF SINBAD THE SAILOR

Sinbad and the Ogre
ISBN 978 0 7496 8559 1*
ISBN 978 0 7496 8571 3

Sinbad and the Whale
ISBN 978 0 7496 8553 9*
ISBN 978 0 7496 8565 2

Sinbad and the Diamond Valley
ISBN 978 0 7496 8554 6*
ISBN 978 0 7496 8566 9

Sinbad and the Monkeys
ISBN 978 0 7496 8560 7*
ISBN 978 0 7496 8572 0

For more *Hopscotch Adventures* and other *Hopscotch* stories, visit:
www.franklinwatts.co.uk

* hardback